Kelly in the *Mirror*

Kelly in the **Mirror**

Martha M. Vertreace

Illustrated by
Sandra Speidel

Albert Whitman & Company, Morton Grove, Illinois

The illustrations are pastel.
The typeface for the text is Palatino.
Designed by Lucy Smith.

Text © 1993 by Martha M. Vertreace.
Illustrations © 1993 by Sandra Speidel.
Published in 1993 by Albert Whitman & Company,
6340 Oakton Street, Morton Grove, Illinois 60053-2723.
Published simultaneously in Canada by
General Publishing, Limited, Toronto.
All rights reserved. Printed in the U.S.A.
10 9 8 7 6 5 4 3 2 1

Library of Congress Cataloging-in-Publication Data
Vertreace, Martha M.
Kelly in the mirror / Martha Vertreace; illustrated by Sandra Speidel.
p.   cm.
Summary: A young girl feels sad that she
doesn't look like anyone in her family—until
she finds a photograph album in the attic.
ISBN 0-8075-4152-4
[1. Family—Fiction. 2. Mothers and daughters—Fiction.]
I. Speidel, Sandra, ill.   II. Title.
PZ7.V6134Ke 1993   92-22655
                                                              CIP
                                                              AC

For my parents, Walter and Modena Vertreace,
and my cousin William Edward Kendrick. M.M.V.

To Jennifer Williams,
and to my daughter, Zoe, my magic mirror. S.S.

Kelly hears Mamma
talking to Grandma on the phone.
"Oh, yes," Mamma says, "everyone
thinks that Bryan looks like his daddy
and Erin looks like me!"

Kelly watches Bryan lean
against Daddy.
"Look!" says Daddy.
"He even has my eyes!"
Bryan looks at Daddy
with big, brown eyes,
and Daddy looks at Bryan
with big, brown eyes.

Kelly watches Erin
hug Mamma's neck.
"Look!" says Mamma.
"Erin's eyebrows curve
just like mine!"
And it's true. Kelly sees two faces
with crescent-moon eyebrows.

"I wonder who I look like,"
Kelly thinks.
She goes to the hall mirror,
which shows her from head to knees.
She sees a turned-up nose
and high cheekbones
and two long braids with ribbons.
"My eyes are small,
not large like Daddy's.
My eyebrows are straight,
not curved like Mamma's.
Maybe the only person
I look like is me!"
She says this softly, so no one else
will know it makes her very sad.

Kelly goes upstairs
to the attic, her special place
to be alone.
In the attic are spaces to explore,
and by the time she looks
at everything, she is almost
happy again.

She touches
the broken sewing machine
her great-grandma owned.
Mamma's is electric—
press a lever on the floor,
and it runs like magic! So easy!
Great-Grandma's has a heavy treadle.
Mamma told her that it worked
when Great-Grandma rocked the treadle
with her foot.

She finds Grandpa's camera,
a plain black box without dials
or numbers. He took pictures long ago
of special days, like when Mamma
was a rose in the school play.
Daddy's camera is fancy,
with different lenses.
Sometimes he changes from one
to another.

In a box in the corner
is Mamma's teddy bear.
He's Kelly's favorite,
even though he has no fur.
She scoops him up and kisses him.
He doesn't have a name—
he's just Bear.

She opens the clothes chest.
There's Mamma's old cap—
brown wool, with a fuzzy pompom.
It just fits!
She finds Mamma's sweater
that Grandma knitted
when Mamma was a little girl herself.
The sweater is navy blue
with white patch pockets.
Mamma once told Kelly that
sometimes Grandma slipped
peppermint wheels into the pockets.
To Kelly's surprise,
the sweater fits perfectly, too.

She stares at herself in the attic mirror.
"Now," she says,
"I don't even look like myself."
But no one hears her say that,
except Bear.

Beneath more old clothes
she finds the corner of a leather book
she's never seen before.

A photograph album!

Kelly plops down
on the green velvet couch
with Bear and the album.

"Kelly?"
"I'm up here, Mamma!"
Kelly hears the squish
of Mamma's tennis shoes on the stairs.
Mamma is surprised to see Kelly
in the old sweater and hat.
"How different you look!" she says,
and Kelly feels sad again.

Then Mamma puts her arm around Kelly
and looks at her for a long time.
Suddenly Mamma smiles.
"I have an idea," she says.
"Let's look at the pictures together."

Kelly opens the album.
"That's my tenth birthday party,"
Mamma says.
Kelly sees five little girls
blowing red balloons
near a big white cake with ten candles.
But Mamma's face is hidden
behind a pretty box with a red ribbon.

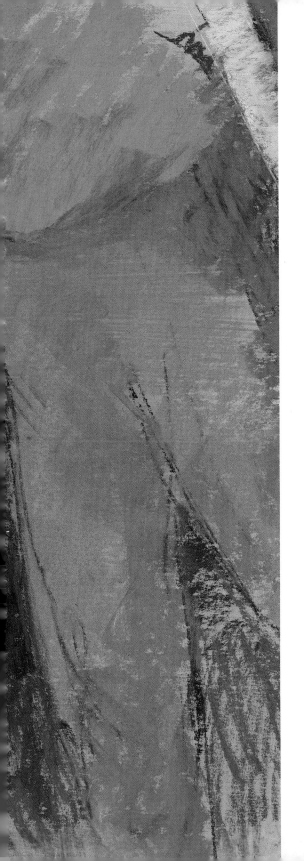

Mamma turns the page.
"Here I am at a carnival with Grandpa,"
she says. "I love merry-go-rounds!"

Kelly sees Mamma at the fairgrounds,
holding pink cotton candy
with one hand,
Grandpa's hand with the other.
But the picture is blurry,
so Kelly can't see Mamma's face.

"And this is me
on the first day of school."
There stands a little girl
with two long braids with ribbons,
like Kelly's,
with a turned-up nose,
like Kelly's,
and high cheekbones,
like Kelly's.
She is wearing the sweater and hat
that Kelly has on,
and she is even holding Bear—
with fur!

"She looks like me!" Kelly says.
"I mean, I look like her!
I look like you, Mamma,
when you were a little girl!
I look just like you!"

Daddy's feet squeak on the stairs,
with Bryan's and Erin's feet
making little squeaks.
"What are you two doing up here?"
Daddy asks.

"We're looking at pictures
of Mamma and Grandma
and Grandpa!" Kelly says.

"Why, Kelly," Daddy says,
"you look just like your mother
in these photos!"

"I have an idea,"
Kelly says with a big smile.
"Everyone can put on something
from this chest,
then Daddy can take our picture!"

Daddy goes to his den
to get his camera
and tripod.

Bryan slips on the red plaid shirt
Daddy used to wear around the house.

Erin finds her mother's T-shirt
with I LOVE NEW YORK on the front.

Mamma puts on Great-Grandma's
felt tam.

Daddy laughs when he sees them all
standing together.
He sets up his camera
and puts it on automatic
so he can be in the picture.

"Say cheese!" Mamma says.

James Plath

Martha M. Vertreace is poet-in-residence and associate professor of English at Kennedy-King College, Chicago, Illinois. She has published two adult collections of poetry, *Second House from the Corner*, which contains photographs from her trips to Ireland, and *Under a Cat's-Eye Moon*. She also writes fiction and essays.

Ideas for stories and poems often come to Martha while she is traveling. *Kelly in the Mirror*, which is her first children's book, was revised while she was at the Hawthornden International Writers' Retreat in Lasswade, Midlothian, Scotland.

Martha was born in Washington, D.C. She shares her Chicago home with her three cats, Beauty, Beast, and Black-Cat, who all declined to be photographed.

Sandra Speidel's pastels have won acclaim at the Society of Illustrators' exhibits in New York and San Francisco. Sandra is a member of the faculty of the Academy of Art College in San Francisco and shows her work in several galleries. This is the fifth book she has illustrated for children.

Sandra lives in California with her daughter, Zoe.

Becky Osgood